How many PIG books have you
.ea.. .i.re .. .. ... .. .. .. .. .. ... .... s.
best to read them in this order:

7. **Pig** and the Ice-cream Cake

8. **Pig** Skives off School

9. **Pig** is a Blue Baboon's Bottom

10. Super**Pig**!

11. **Pig** and the Baldy Cat

12. **Pig** Leaves Home (for a bit)

13. **Pig** tells a Whopping Great Fib

14. **Pig** is Hairy Snotter

15. **Pig** and the Rainbow Hair

16. **Pig** and the Big Quiz

17. **Pig** gets Angry

18. **Pig**'s Season's Finale    ... and more!

PIG is Hairy Snotter
by Barbara Catchpole
Illustrated by Dynamo

Published by Ransom Publishing Ltd.
Unit 7, Brocklands Farm, West Meon, Hampshire
GU32 1JN, UK
**www.ransom.co.uk**

ISBN     978 178127 536 8
First published in 2015

is

# Hairy Snotter

## Barbara Catchpole

Illustrated by Dynamo

Ransom

Bob was after me! I knew it! He was going to do something horrible! He was smiling, but he was thinking up Bob's Revenge! Da da dah!

I was leaving town.

It was a good job we were going on the School Surfing Holiday. It was more like the School Falling Off a Manky Old Board Holiday – but at least it was a holiday. And it was free!

I'd won it for being in the Head Teacher's Secret Toilet without asking. They said I needed a Roll Model. That's not a toilet roll. I think it's like a ham roll, but different.

Although I told them I eat rolls all the time (not toilet rolls - that would be weird. I'm not weird).

Mum gets the cheap end-of-day bread rolls from her job at Tescos.

I kept a diary when I was on holiday. We had to, for homework. Diaries are not at all girly, like Raj said.

Raj didn't come on holiday because his mum said she didn't want him to get a beach bum.

What's a beach bum? Whatever it is, I want one! It sounds a dead cool thing to have! Maybe there are beach bum shops where you can buy them!

All these bums lined up on the shelves and you choose the one you would like to wear for a while.

Raj's mum said her Raj didn't need to learn to surf – he was going to be a doctor when he left school. He wouldn't have any time for surfing.

'My Rajesh will help the whole world with his discoveries.'

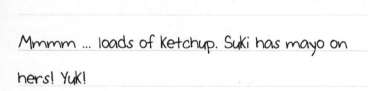

I stopped listening and started thinking about chips.

Mmmm ... loads of ketchup. Suki has mayo on hers! Yuk!

'My Rajesh will be a great doctor.'

I wonder if they're doing scraps. I love scraps!

'My Rajesh will play cricket for India.'

Brilliant smell of hot vinegar.

'He will buy a
big house for
his dear
mother.'

Chip sandwich –
melting butter.

'He will have lots of children. I will be a grandmother. They will grow up to be doctors. Then they will have children and ... '

'Mum! Mum!'

Raj gave his mum a little shake. He loves her to bits, but when she bangs on about him getting

married and the grandchildren (and sometimes great-grandchildren) he usually stops her. If he can!

I was still thinking about chips.

'Anyway that is why my Rajesh is not going surfing – so he will not become a beach bum. No offence.'

I really missed Raj on the trip (in a manly way, of course).

Anyhow – here is my diary! Sorry about the ketchup on it. It's been on the kitchen table for a week. And ignore the bit Harry chewed.

I think he might have eaten some of Day Two.
There's something on Day Four too — I'm not
sure if it's a raisin or hamster poo.

## Day One

Number of times people sick:     12

Number of kids wanting their mum:     4

Number of times Sir said 'I'm taking you

all back to the school':     5

I am on the coach. Lee Wong's mum made him take sickness pills. He was sick in the hood of Dean Gosnall's coat before we got to the end of the road. (We could still see the school.)

He said:

'Gruaggh!'

Then he said:

'Tablets always make me throw up!'

Then he went:

'Woohurgh! Gruaggh! Woohurgh!'

Then the smell made us all want to throw up
and we had to go back to the school to clean up.

Dean had to empty his hood. The driver was
angry and said some bad words and Mr
Strange told him off.

Then we got back on the coach and ate our packed lunches because our stomachs were empty.

Lee felt sick again and Sir gave him a paper bag. Now Sir is holding a paper bag full of Lee sick and the driver won't stop the coach, he's just driving along singing a happy song.

I don't think Mr Strange is too pleased. He is holding a bag of cold sick (OK, it might still be warm) and I expect he is missing Miss Hardcastle.

Did I tell you I saw them getting kissy-kissy smoochy-woochy in the English stockroom?

I miss Mum and Raj and I think I'm feeling a bit sick ...

Got to stop writing now!

## Day Two

Number of times people sick:     0

Number of times I fell off surfboard:    27

Number of times Sir said 'I'm taking you
all back to the school':    4 (all to Zac).


It was freezing on the beach. Instead of
answering our names, we were each given a
number and we have to 'sound off'. I am
number seven and I forgot it three times. In
the end Mr
Strange did it
for me because
he said:

   'We will
   never get
   into the
water at this rate.'

 He was right because
it took us ages to get
into the wet suits.
We kept standing on
one leg and falling
over, and getting
sand inside the suits.

Then when you do get the suit on, you can't get
the bit between your legs to pull up. There seems
to be too much suit in some places and not enough
in other places – quite important places, too!

The surfing guy and Mr Strange just wet
themselves laughing. They were no help at all.
I missed my mum.

Best bit of the day: Zac Zwing told Sky a crab had crawled into his ear. Zac said he had seen it - a tiny pink crab. Sky started to cry because he thought he could feel it in there.

Then Zac said he saw it waving a claw out of Sky's nose. Sky told Sir and Sir banged on for ages about why it was impossible, with pictures of the ear drawn in the sand and stuff.

Then Zac said:

'Saw it again!'

and Sky screamed.

Ryan Robbins won't eat anything because he only likes sausages.

We put my plastic poo in Mr Strange's bed and now he won't let me have it back.

I told him my mum would come down the school to complain, but she won't. She's fed up with me and that poo.

# Day Three

Number of times people sick:    0

Number of times I fell off surfboard:    34

Number of times Sir threatened to take us

back:    2

They've made me number one because Mr

Strange says:

'Life's too short'.

I fell off my board thirty-four times today
and Sir said he was proud of me! I don't know
why – falling off things is dead easy. Sometimes
I fall off my chair in the classroom. I reckon
I could fall off anything.

I am feeling a bit stressy because Suki sent me
a text saying:

    Gt back!

    Fings r happening!

I am still worried
because of Bob and his
Revenge. All I did was
tell him three giant
mega-lies and try to ruin

his life! What would be Bob's revenge for a
little thing like that?

Suki might be winding me up though. Mum says
she is a real 'wind-up merchant'. Things Suki has
told me:

Hamsters turn
into rats after
six months.

Baked beans turn your hair red.

If it rains too much, the sky falls down.
(I was three when she said that.
I wouldn't go out in the rain for weeks.)

Snakes can come up through the toilet.
(I am still a bit worried about this one,
but Mum says if they did, Suki wouldn't
ever go to the bathroom – and she spends
whole days in there.)

Suki says telling lies makes pimples on your
tongue. (I am very worried about that one.)

Bob is really a nice guy, isn't he? He is, isn't he?

# Day Four

Number of times people sick:    0

Number of times I fell off surfboard:    37

(a record! I'm definitely getting really
good at it - falling off, that is).

Number of times Sir said he would take us
back if we didn't behave:    11 (another
record!).


We are all tired and fed up and Mr Strange is
ratty because last night I had a nightmare
that Harry turned into a rat and came up our
toilet. I screamed and woke everyone up at
three o'clock in the morning.


I still can't stand up on my surfboard, but I

can sort of crouch down. And it means I'm nearer the sea when I fall off.

Today Sir drove the minibus thirty miles to buy sausages. Ryan ate seventeen in one go and did a huge burp. (I bet that isn't all he did!)

Now this is the tricky bit. Stop eating those crisps and listen up!

I have written two Day Fives and two Day Sixes. One is for school, because I don't want them knowing all my business. The other is super-secret and just for you. I don't mind you knowing. And Raj. You and Raj are my best mates.

## School Day Five

Number of times people sick:    2

(after feast)

Number of times I fell off board:    only 9!

Not worth taking us back now!

Today I stood up on my surfboard for at least a count of three. It was awesome and everybody saw it!

Tonight we are going to have a midnight feast

with stuff we have taken from meals and hidden up our sleeves, because we are going home tomorrow.

Ryan has four cold sausages and I have a bit of chicken and a potato.

They're a bit fluffy, but I'm going to eat them anyway!

Dean's got a torch (to see with – not to eat!).

# Secret Day Five

(for your eyes only – secret spy version)

I got a really weird phone call from Suki:

'Listen, Pig! Mum says I've got to pick you up from the coach when it gets in, but I don't want to!

'Perhaps I can make Kim do it. Why do I

29

have to do everything? It's like so unfair!
By the way, all your stuff is gone and
Rajesh has got your duvet cover! See ya!'

I tried to phone her back, but she wasn't
answering.

I didn't like my ratty old duvet cover anyway.
It had the Spice Girls on it and their eyes were
always looking at you and their smiles were

creepy. But why had Raj got it? And what did she mean by 'all your stuff is gone'? Where had all my stuff gone? And did she mean ... EVERYthing?

This had to be Evil Bob's work! He had to be stopped!

## School Day Six

Number of times people sick:   7

(on coach)

Then we went home again and it was nice to see my family. The End.

# Secret Day Six

Don't tell them at school what happened! I feel a bit silly now, but at the time it was horrible!

On the coach back, Lee Wong was even more sick than before. I think he'd forgotten to take any tablets. This time he was sick down Zac Zwing's neck. I know – brilliant!

He had just stood up and said:

'Sir I feel sick,'

and Zac had just turned
round to say 'Ha! Ha!'
and then when Zac
turned back, Lee was
sick all down his back.
Well, between his back
and his clothes, most of
it. I think some went
down the back of his
trousers, too.

Anyway, I got a call from Suki. I couldn't hear
all that well because everyone was shouting.

'I can't get you from school like I said to Mum, so just lug your stuff home, bro – I'll be here. Got things to do. Oh – my – God! Just wait until you see – I'm SO sorry for you!'

Suki didn't sound sorry – she sounded like she was wetting herself laughing.

Then she hung up. I phoned back, but it went to voicemail.

What was going on?

Then we sang songs on the coach. We sang 'She'll be wearing pink pyjamas when she comes,' and then Mr Strange sang 'She'll be sick down Zac's back when she comes.'

That made us all laugh. Except Lee and Zac.

Everybody else had someone to meet them, but Sir gave me a lift home.

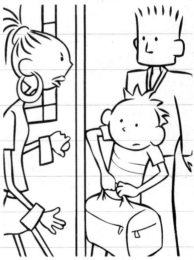

Suki opened the door.
She said:

'Thank you, Sir.'

Sir taught Suki too –
back in the days when

there were blackboards, chalk and dinosaurs.

Suki stood and watched while I ran up to my room. I just stopped in the doorway and looked.

My stuff was all gone!

Where were my football posters and the broken bowling pin the bloke gave me? Where were my fart bombs? Not under my bed, because there was a cot in the middle of the room. There was a heater! I could have done with that!

But no bed, no Spice Wrinklies duvet cover – no room for Pig.

'Come down here!'

Suki was grinning from ear to ear. She showed me the cupboard under the stairs. All that was in there was a light bulb hanging from a wire.

She said:

'Unpack your sleeping bag, this is where you sleep now. Under the stairs, like Hairy

Snotter or whatever he's called. You made Bob mad and now he is getting his own back. All your stuff went on eBay. You won't like him now – he's paying you back, big time!'

and she laughed and laughed. Her blue eye gunk ran down her face.

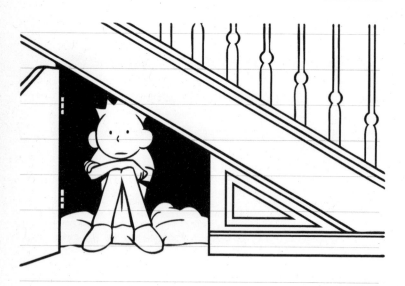

I put my things in the cupboard and crawled in. There were little hamster poos everywhere. Harry uses the cupboard as a safe house. We usually keep the hoover there – he likes to get stuck up the pipe.

I sat in the cupboard on my sleeping bag for a while. I could still hear Suki laughing outside. I didn't cry of course, but some of the dust from the floor got in my eyes. Suki shut the door and it was dark and cold in there.

How could Mum do this, I thought? Perhaps she loves Bob more than she loves me. I had a big hurt feeling inside my tummy. I curled up on my bag and went to sleep.

# Welcome home

I heard Mum's voice in the hall:

    'Where is he? Where's my little guy?'

Suki shouted:

    'Bye! Must go!'

I heard the front door slam.

I came out of the cupboard under the stairs and just stood there. I hated it in there! I wanted my room back! I was even sadder than Harry Potter without any magic.

    'Pig! What are you doing in there? Have you seen it?'

I said:

'Yes, it's a great cupboard. I like the light
bulb.'


'No, not the cupboard, you doofus – your
new room!'


Raj and Bob followed in after Mum, both talking

at once. Then Mum hugged me, turned me around and put her nice soft hands over my eyes. What was going on?

 She turned me around again and pushed me a bit and took her hands off my eyes and I was in the Room We Never Use.

And ... WOW! Whoooa! It was amazing – just so cool. My bed and my stuff had been moved. My bed had a new duvet – bright blue!

(Raj had been given the Spice Girls one, but he

said his Mum wasn't keen on it and he had to show off like mad to get it on his bed. He said he wasn't going to be a doctor if he couldn't have a Spice Girls duvet and slammed a door.)

It was the walls that were amazing though. It turns out Bob had spent all week painting them. They were half under the sea, with a huge octopus  in one corner and loads of fish and stuff: jellyfish and seahorses and starfish and sharks with big mouths and sharp teeth and a clown fish like in the cartoons.

The top half was above the sea and it had me surfing - hands out, dead cool, and Harry was there too! Bob had painted him on a tiny surfboard. I looked like a Cool Surf Dude and Harry looked like a Cool Surf Dude with Fur.

The sun was in the sky and there were bright red and green parrots flying about.

I couldn't say a word. I just stood,
gob-smacked, with my mouth hanging open.

Mum said:

'Don't you like it?'

I bet she was worried I wasn't going to say
'thank you'.

'It's kickin'! It's incredible! It's awesome!
Where did you get the money?'

'Robbed a bank!'

It turned out that the TV people gave Mum
some money after she went to tell them 'nicely

and politely and quietly' what she thought about them putting me on telly when I was skiving school. I bet she had a right go!

They gave some money to Raj too. His mum is saving it for when he is a doctor. He might need a new white coat or something.

Mum gave me a huge hug and said she missed me and I think she cried a bit.

Bob was very weird and shook my hand. What is he like?

Bob said:

'Thank you for telling me the truth, Pig. That was brave! I was stupid to believe you in the first place.'

Mum said:

'Let me get this right, Bob.'

I watched a program on telly once with this really old guy talking about birds. The mum-bird fluffed itself up to look big and scare off another bird who wanted to eat her eggs.

My mum can do that - sort of fluff herself up to look really angry. That's what she did now - a huge, angry Mum bird.

Bob looked scared.

Mum said:

> 'Let – me – just – get – this right. You were stupid to believe anyone else would want to take me out? So you don't think I am gorgeous or clever or fit? Stupid! Yes, you ARE stupid, Robert Sidebottom!'

Bob stood there, looking more like a goldfish than ever. He said:

> 'Susan ... I didn't ... I can't ... I don't ... I am so sorry!'

Mum was so angry she was shaking. No she wasn't. I knew what was going to happen now!

48

It was like an
explosion! Her big
laugh boomed round
our hall. She was
winding him up. Suki
had learned from
my mum! Mum had
taught Suki all she
knew.

Mum said to me:

'Why did you go into the cupboard, my little
dingbat?'

I told her what Suki had said. Mum shook her
head sadly.

'I love you Pig. You gotta trust me!'

I felt a bit ashamed. Bob looked ashamed too, and she wasn't even talking to him! Then she cheered up a bit.

'Where did you put those fart bombs, Bob?'

'Under the bed.'

I suppose Bob's not so bad.

Mum said:

'You know what to do, Pig!'

Mum and Bob went and bought chips and I went up to Suki's room with a box of fart bombs.

I let off six and shut the door carefully.

It smelled like two elephants had farted in there – just after winning a baked-bean eating competition.

Pig's Revenge! Wa-ha-ha!

The next **PIG** book is

**PIG**

and the

Rainbow Hair

## About the author

Barbara Catchpole was a teacher for thirty years and enjoyed every minute. She has three sons of her own who were always perfectly behaved and never gave her a second of worry.

Barbara also tells lies.